A CLASSIC

~ MICKEY MOUSE ~

TALE

Designed by Scott Piehl

Copyright © 2018 Disney Enterprises, Inc.

All rights reserved.

Published by Disney Press, an imprint of Disney Book Group.

No part of this book may be reproduced or transmitted in any form or by any means,
electronic or mechanical, including photocopying, recording, or by any information
storage and retrieval system, without written permission from the publisher.

For information address Disney Press,
1200 Grand Central Avenue, Glendale, California 91201.

Printed in the United States of America

First Hardcover Edition, January 2018

Library of Congress Control Number: 2017914124

1 3 5 7 9 10 8 6 4 2

ISBN 978-1-368-02331-3

FAC-008598-17321

For more Disney Press fun,
visit www.disneybooks.com

A CLASSIC MICKEY MOUSE TALE

The Sorcerer's Apprentice

Adapted by
Brooke Vitale

Illustrated by the
Disney Storybook Art Team

DISNEP PRESS

Los Angeles · New York

ONCE there was a great sorcerer who knew everything there was to know about magic.

He brewed potions that could make camels talk.

He transformed pebbles into rubies and diamonds.

He made the stars shoot across the sky and burst onto the ground wherever he directed them.

THE Sorcerer had a wonderful hat. When he wore his hat, all he had to do was think magic and it would happen.

He could think about a butterfly and it would appear. But only the Sorcerer knew the magic words that would make it disappear.

THE Sorcerer was very busy. He did not have time to tend to his castle and still perform his brilliant magic. So he had a helper.

Mickey did all the work in the castle. He swept the floor. He chopped the wood. He carried the water from the fountain into the castle.

Late one evening, Mickey watched as the Sorcerer cleaned up his workshop and went to bed. Soon Mickey found himself all alone.

WHEN he entered the Sorcerer's workshop, he saw the magic hat sitting on the table. Mickey tried to walk away, but the temptation was too great. He had seen the magic the Sorcerer could perform with the hat, and he longed to have a magic hat of his own.

MICKEY looked at the magic hat.

Ever so slowly, he reached for it.

Ever so gently, he took it off the table.

Ever so carefully, he raised it into the air.

Ever so proudly, he lowered it onto his head.

Finally, he would be a sorcerer, too.

AS Mickey peered around the room, his gaze fell on an old broom leaning against the wall. Suddenly, Mickey knew what his first spell would be.

Mickey did what the Sorcerer always did. He pointed his fingers straight at the broom. At once, the broom began to shake. Its bristles parted, turning into two legs, and it hopped toward Mickey once, and then a second time.

Mickey pointed at the broom again and it sprouted a right arm . . . and then a left arm.

REACHING down, the broom picked up two nearby buckets.

Mickey gestured for the broom to follow him up the steps. The broom did as Mickey commanded.

Mickey led the broom to the fountain and waited for it to fill the buckets. Then Mickey led the broom back down the stairs. Pointing at a large vat, he watched as the broom poured the water inside.

Again and again, the broom marched up the stairs, filled the buckets, and poured the water into the vat.

MICKEY danced around the room.

Doing magic was easy. He would never have

to work again!

But ordering the broom around had made Mickey tired.

He sat down in the Sorcerer's chair. Waving his hand, he

kept the broom working.

Soon Mickey fell sound asleep. He dreamed he was

the greatest sorcerer in the world.

SUDDENLY, something cold and wet hit Mickey. It was a splash of water.

Another splash knocked Mickey out of the chair.

Mickey woke up and looked around. There was water everywhere! While he had slept, the broom had continued filling the vat with water. Now it was overflowing and flooding the room.

MICKEY threw out his hands, commanding the broom to stop. But alas, Mickey only knew how to make the magic start. He did not know how to make it stop. So the broom continued marching up the stairs, filling the buckets, and bringing them back to the vat. Mickey held out his arms, but the broom pushed him down. He grabbed the buckets, but the broom held on tight. Wasn't there any way to stop the broom?

SUDDENLY, Mickey spotted the ax he used to chop the Sorcerer's wood. He grabbed the ax and chopped the broom into bits. Soon there was nothing left but a pile of splinters.

MICKEY relaxed. He was glad that was over. But it *wasn't* over. The bits of wood began to move. Each piece turned into a new broom, and each broom had two new buckets!

THE brooms pushed past Mickey and marched up the stairs. A moment later, the brooms came back down the steps with more water. Mickey tried to hold them back, but they walked right over him. In a great line, they poured more and more water into the vat.

THE water in the room grew deeper and deeper.

It was all Mickey could do to keep himself from being pulled under.

The Sorcerer's book of magic floated by. Mickey grabbed it. He turned page after page after page, looking for the magic words that would stop the brooms.

But as the water began to whirl, Mickey could no longer read the words.

MICKEY hung on to the book as he went around and around in the water, spinning faster and faster in the great whirlpool.

SUDDENLY, a bright light filled the room.

The Sorcerer had returned.

Looking at the water covering his workshop, the Sorcerer knew at once what Mickey had done.

He raised his arms and waved a great command. The water parted and began to disappear. The Sorcerer frowned down at Mickey, then waved his arms again. The brooms and the buckets disappeared. Soon only Mickey's old broom and buckets remained.

MICKEY took off the Sorcerer's hat. Very carefully, he tried to make the magic hat look nice again. Then he gave it back to the Sorcerer.

Mickey smiled shyly at the Sorcerer. But the Sorcerer did not smile back.

MICKEY gave the old broom to the Sorcerer, picked up his buckets, and tried to sneak away. But as he went, the Sorcerer gave Mickey's bottom a good hard smack with the broom!

Mickey quickly ran off to do his work. He had learned his lesson: never start something you don't know how to finish.